Brendan Connell was born in Santa Fe, New Mexico, in 1970. His works of fiction include *The Architect* (PS Publishing, 2012), *Lives of Notorious Cooks* (Chômu Press, 2012), *Miss Homicide Plays the Flute* (Eibonvale Press, 2013), *Cannibals of West Papua* (Zagava, 2015), *Against the Grain Again: The Further Adventures of Des Esseintes* (Tartarus Press, 2021), and *Heqet* (Egaeus Press, 2022). As editor he has worked on various projects, including *The World in Violet: An Anthology of English Decadent Poetry* (Snuggly Boos, 2022), and *The Neo-Decadent Cookbook* (Eibonvale Press, 2020), which was co-edited by Justin Isis. As translator his efforts include *Alcina and Other Stories* (Snuggly Books, 2019), by Guido Gozzano, which was co-translated by his wife Anna.

BRENDAN CONNELL

SPELLS

THIS IS A SNUGGLY BOOK

ISBN: 978-1-64525-120-0

The section of this book titled "Drops of Poison" was previously published by Eibonvale Press in 2013, in a chapbook limited to 26 copies. The section of this book titled "Curious Births to Light the Universe" was previously published by Eibonvale Press in 2017, in a chapbook limited to 50 copies. The sections "Vegetable Spells" and "Papiliones in Sordibus" are original to *Spells*.

for Anna

CONTENTS

SPELLS

VEGETABLE SPELLS

WHEN THE CHILDREN

When the children, their hands and mouths stained brightly, returned home that evening they all brought with them fruits.

The fruits were large and of a gorgeous shade—no one had ever seen their like before; and their flesh was delicious.

"In the heart of the forest there is a tree, and from it we picked these."

Many then went to that place and, discovering the tree, picked its fruit, ate and went jolly, kissing each other and moving their bodies in delight.

Their spit was foam.

Even the most masculine had become androgynous.

Some spoke in languages they did not know; some prophecies; some thought they were centaurs or the moans of demonesses; and then hypnotized they went.

They let the sun strike them.

They pleaded for its sparks to pierce them.

The tree was gone, but in remembering it, in telling of it and reciting its story, the people hoped thereby to gain their salvation.

"Remember the radiance . . ."

"The globules were animating."

". . . our mission!"

JACOB, THE BLACKSMITH

Jacob, the blacksmith, made horseshoes and sickles, hinges and nails.

He was greatly respected, since his arms were strong, his beard thick, and the products of his hammer much needed.

Before dawn spread her transparent wings he would light his coke, and he was still at it when the hard hooves of night were known.

He worked and lived at the town wall, by the principal entrance, where the capers grew, and one night, when the moon was full and the gaze of the stars was mild, as he was closing the door to his forge and was about to enter his dwelling, he saw a small man with a purple hat walk by.

A stranger?

That man walked into the wall and disappeared, and this occurrence made Jacob marvel.

When he slept, he dreamed of frothing liquids and forests growing thick with herbs and the aching of lost loves.

The next night he again saw the man with the purple hat walk into the wall, and the same thing happened two nights after that, and those nights, also, were filled with sweet-sad dreams that caused him to awake with tears on his cheeks.

"There is something that remains unknown," he said to himself.

And with this thought he took up a spade, a spade he had fashioned himself, and he dug in the spot by the wall and found bones, but what bones?

IT WAS DURING THE TIME

It was during the time of the coming and going of kings.

They, those golden men, lived in tents and used their seed wisely.

The temples were beneath the ground; no place was more cool than those fortified depths.

And that was where some special beasts lived, some beneath-men, where in frenzies they crawled and hopped.

Unable to break down the barriers of mutism, they only croaked, growled, or barked.

The temples were dark and had strange fragrances; and back behind the altars, naked, semi-sexless, the beasts knelt, with their intent only on *it*.

That was their allotted occupation.

And the gods found it good.

And the gods, there were more than nine of them, took joy in their dirty hair.

Then the minds of the kings were lost.

They made many men go the way of death.

They abandoned their tents and resided in large palaces where the sound of tortured slaves mixed with that of lascivious song.

Bastards whose beards were painted red with evil entered and desecrated the temples.

"What is that?" said Inurta-šarru-usur, son of Aššur-eriba and prefect of Nabû-šimanni, who, having been taken up with quite a few lawsuits, hadn't been to the capitol in a while.

The king laughed and showed his fangs.

"That is unnamable," said he. "They are all the rage. This one I bought at the market for eight talents of *minas* of silver—more expensive than the best camel, to be sure—but its hump is larger as well."

"And its use?"

"If you knew what I DO with it, the pleasure I derive from bending and DOING things to it, your envy would be as long as the Deqlat—as long as that endless river."

"It seems that you keep it well groomed."

"It is bathed in perfume and fed on sweetmeats, honey-dipped dates and pies of butter throughout the day, so that at night . . ."

"You were never one to leave good land unploughed."

But the gods control all destinies.

And it came to pass that they, in their sympathy and benevolence, gave the *unnamable* a thirst.

And that thirst was not for water or wine.

It was so *endless* that, listening to the midnight voice of Sapunâ, the slave woman, who transmitted secrets and mysteries through her melodious whispers, it drained a thousand lakes.

And so it came to pass that when the bowmen came and filled the land with arrows, the unnamable, having learned greatly in life's school, avoided that fate.

Their temples they then built in high places and they were soon the Genii of Perception.

The rest is broken away.

THE VALLEY WAS QUIET

The valley was quiet and the evening cool and the difficulties of the world were far away and the bees were fat around the lavender and the apples shone, each one a gravitational world.

The garden was the birthplace of vegetables; and Signora Wistinghausen lay in her chair, her eyes enamel, her skin eggshells, her hair Egyptian jasper.

She had eaten a piece of bread and a piece of cheese and a bowl of lettuce, lettuce that had grown in her patch, and she was a woman who had had in her life both sweet and salt, had drunk of bitter things and tasted pungent flavors.

The ores of the heart are sometimes lead and sometimes gold; and the mind of Signora Wistinghausen was mennige and silver, amethyst and juicy green, and then the evening

grew somewhat darker and the sky was painted a most curious shade, like a dreaming lake.

"You have given us infinite love," they said.
"The roots of the trees stretch down into hell,
but the monsters there will never touch you;
you will never be touched by violent spears.
Through your kindness, your mind has
reached the third dimension, and each of your
fingers is attached to a different star, which
will pull in full grace when you wish, and you
can be the flying maiden—can look down on
the forests wide and the swift-drawn rivers.
Sweet milk has been taken from your breasts,
tender touches from your hands, contributary
hymns from your lips. Your footsteps are little
leaves and your teeth are beetles. Do you wish
to see the gifts we have for you, to be given
that key?"

The German vines had covered everything
as had the wormy earth, but before the parade
could properly begin, there were the dragon
scales and a vibration of sound, and then
René, her small-eyed lover, was there, telling
her she should come inside, and wondering
why she had been lying in the garden.

"It is important never to listen to devils,"
he said. "Not every object with wings is an
angel and sometimes it is necessary to exor-

cise one's surroundings. Eating dead things is obligatory for both pleasure and knowledge. I have made pacts with the rays of the moon and fangs of the bat. When I was younger I cauterized men who had lost their arms and legs. I juggled with eyeballs and sliced off tongues. In the huts sacrifices were made before statues of desiccated grasses and one could hear the trembling screams of goats. Bodies came out from their graves and I watched them wander for seven years. The padlocks of all doors fell away and I became invisible. With the blood of beasts I painted your name on heated breasts and with crocodile teeth I gnawed on succulent bones. Now we, my dear, chained together by love, must mingle our bodies, distilling our emotions with boggy sweat."

The deeper mysteries remain concealed to the swaying of the valley's golden grain; and things were hurried; and that night the stars sat still in the heavens, as if they were decorations on a black blanket.

VALENTINA HAD A FEAR

Valentina had a fear of axes.

Valentina Osterwalder, that caretaker of hospitality, she feared them so much; and her soul was a scrapbook of terror.

Would an axe one day fall upon her neck or arm?

She had dreams of being headless; of her beautiful brown hair, of shimmering length, soaked in gore.

Her white teeth, in that head, would become so cold.

A lover of walks in the woods, she wept on the day she saw that it had been cut down.

Wept and trembled.

Visions came to her.

Visions terrible, in which blood and sap intertwined and the high-pitched chirp she heard was a scream—nothing like something that would come from the mouth of a bird.

The vital principle—how they had dared to take it!

Her fingers became tense at the thought.

She wandered, barefoot, about her garden in anguish, her toes becoming wet with dew.

Then, when the day had drawn on and the bells of the Chiesa di San Lorenzo had sounded, so that the faithful might hear, she shod herself and set out into the bosque.

She walked quickly and in the quiet dusk arrived.

Its trunk had been segmented into many pieces, and they were there waiting.

Waiting for what?

"You, you hero, you," she said, "please forgive me for my cowardice, for my disloyalty to the grove. Next time, it shall not be so. I shall, in fact, in the days that come, put my body, my body of flesh, my only possession, within one of your brothers. I shall, without causing the least damage (for I am soft), go far, deep within, within the wood, feeling it firm about me—retaining me in exultation. And so, when the butchers arrive, with their weapons and tools, if they dare cut him, it is me, also, who they will cut—and they will sever me in two. And, in such a case, we shall fall together, our blood and sap mingled—but my emotions shall last for eternity."

DROPS OF POISON

VIPEROUS POISON

Viperous poison, you smooth-sliding liquid,
what could one do with you?

When a child, I walked along a forest path,
mind lost in caterpillar dreams. About to set
down my happy foot, I noticed a giant serpent stretched out beneath it, from one side
of the trail to the next. Slowly I stepped back
and ran away. When I returned, much later, it
was gone, to my sorrow.

SUCH WEALTH ENOUGH

Such wealth enough to make one spit with closed eyes impoverished sympathy. Mothers are loved by the poor.

She was blonde.

Blonde as a light-bulb, dandelion, the freshest piss of coreopsis—some princess disgorged from a jackal's beak—and she was full up with the same crude emotions that almost destroyed the century in which she was born.

She hated her mother, bathing in feathers nebulas drenched in the darkness of negative matter. Pearls piled into plateaus. Quicksand of gold. Monkeys vomit silver pebbles and naked boys drown themselves in the juice of platinum.

So then the news came. The queen's body was paraded through the empty desert.

Daylight came too soon.

And the princess inherited emerald camels, diamond-studded weapons, jewelled nooses, old crowns and Mandarin-speaking parrots, and her response to all this was to have her navel removed.

GRIPPING TENDRILS

Gripping tendrils; clear-eyed flowers. It was morning glories that I cut down and cooked up, with Aqua vitae, leeched the plant of its properties and solidified its essence into a rank and sticky tar. I loaded some into a sepiolite pipe carved to resemble the head of Zeus—Deus—God—and applying a match to it, puffed away, a sizzling sound. Some pornographic sweet taste dripped onto my tongue.

Disgusting nymph! I am rolling on the ground avoiding the acicularity of your nipples which stab at me like scimitars and in my deep champagne austerity I wish to grab them, on them impale my wayward emotions, which like minnows thread their way through the shallows of silence.

LONG AGO

Long ago there were no humans on the earth, only animals.

Instead of rolling and playing games together they prowled and played vicious pranks until their fur was clotted with blood.

And these—these wolves and prowling tigers, malicious rodents and brutal apes—these promiscuous, scratching creatures were reborn, not as desperate phantoms but as plain men.

ERGOT OF RYE

Ergot of rye you might find amusing but after a while it felt like hell. The battling laughter pushed me into a corner and I stood biting my own chin and walking along his leg dropped off and two days later fingers began to fall.

My imagination is no longer obedient, a cross-eyed bull charging down a devexity.

Hunched biting myself. They are all holding hands, damned them! What a torment, to suddenly realize I am the plaything of phantoms, a sponge being pulled apart, a random eddy of inconsequence.

EVERY NIGHT

Every night he would drink and weep. He collected his tears in a jar and when he had enough threw a large cocktail party. Only the richest most affluent citizens were invited.

He put a few drops in each drink and after they had been consumed everyone began to strangle each-other.

MY HEART

My heart is like an apple that birds come and feed on, some core hanging in the cold wind beneath the spasms of clouds. My eyes see the thin legs of old courtesans who were once beautiful—the regal couches, scented wines and mad twitter of flutes as sunbeams glance by candid pillars and flies cluster on fruit; like a galley slave, whipped by leather, with foaming mouth like foaming waves, who at night is taken to perform ruttish exercises with some obscene centurion, or to fornicate with fish before the eyes of a white Madame.

THERE IS A PLANT

There is a plant that, when you touch it, curls up and hides. Its roots act as an antidote to poison, especially the venom of serpents— but unfortunately cannot do away with the dahlias of poverty, which let off their scent in apricot-colored urinals and invite the thick fangs of prophets and demons.

Mithridates experimented a great deal with poisons and their antidotes and also built up an immunity to the former by eating small quantities of all sorts of toxins every day; and so when he finally determined to kill himself, no poison would do the trick and in blue-grey desperation he asked a slave to pierce his life.

YOU SWAMP MIASMA

You swamp miasma, crocodile spawn, rampant episode on knee-deep moss—I shiver every time I bend to you—your necromatic breasts oozing their sour milk and your lips which kissed the beak of that bird called the zhenniao that feeds on nothing but the heads of vipers. The droppings of this bird would eat through iron in just a few days. If you cut off its wings and left them in wine, the wine would become poisonous.

Someone once served Wang Chuyi such wine and it had no effect on him. But he was, after all, an immortal.

THE BEAUTY OF THINGS

The beauty of things that drip cannot be out-done by either sleeping flowers or powerful eloquence—the glossy lines of pride which are less sweet than a radish sprinkled with salt.

But let us speak of glory.

It is an old man without teeth who wants to rub his gums over your nose as he mumbles about owls and mice or a mediocre accuser who brays of their own achievements or a battlefield covered with corpses whose eyes are pecked out by crows.

In early fall I pull the blankets tight around me, anticipating the cold that is soon to come.

DATURA

Datura, I wish you to be happy.

I wish to place gold at your ivory feet and give you my superficies on which you could lavish your deliriums.

Your aroma makes me dizzy; you offer me your babies to eat and I blink rapidly as I gobble a few down, in raging intoxication now copulating with a well-oiled frying pan, horror of skull cups and citrus fruits and four-headed swans that sing like storm clouds.

Yes, I wish you to be happy. Together we crawl across the carpet which is rough and rips the fingers from my hands.

I KNEW A MAN

I knew a man who bragged much, but did little, and the little he did had best been left undone.

We were sitting in a café when bells began to land on him until he was completely covered.

Nothing I could do but stroll away.

RADIANT HEROES

Radiant heroes; let me speak of heroes—of those who eat henbane and while intoxicated cause disturbances or, shirtless, sell human brains by the roadside as a tonic while they snack on wax of the ears and gulp down treacle posset mixed with centipedes and white vitriol.

There was an old man who wrote poems to the exclusion of all else. He forgot his wife and daughter. He forgot sobriety.

Poems.

There are many good ones, with turbans of candy, a distant parade of lost soldiers and the fawning taste of bark.

The radiant heroes smoking opium in tiny rooms in Taghazout and hashish adulterated with henna and sitting beneath cypress trees on the California coast high on white dove letting their tongues hang into the sea froth and reflecting on the works of God and those in Loughborough or Pontypool dreaming of otter testicles, long since disappeared due to the use of chlorinated hydrocarbon pesticides.

SMELLING TAR

Smelling tar I feel dizzy and it reeks of assonance and radiance, of comedies and zeal—of the world's indifference.

Immortals use amulets, as do heroes, to ward off evil ghosts, predators, drooling wolves in the black—they can take your body.

If you sleep on the mountain and wish to avoid harm, then make a sleeping-on-mountain plaque and hang it up near you. Whatever wood is easily at hand can be used, though that of fruit trees and pines should be considered especially efficacious.

If you have great skill in drawing, that is best. Next best is to have no skill in drawing.

Paint on the wood a figure with six arms. In the hand of at least one, there should be a dagger. This figure is the protector whose name I shall not write. He stops dragons using bundles of golden leaves; melts tigers;

blocks ghosts who swallow swallow swallow; terminates old winds.

There was a man named Mr. Su who used such a plaque. After making it he bowed twenty-one times.

While in the mountains it is best to pick oyster mushrooms. Do not pick *Amanita muscaria* or set up camp near them.

LOVE

Love, you fed it to me in painful drops, an orgasmic honey that changed my body into that of a dog. And now I bark and shiver, growl and lick any friendly hand.

But my shape-shifting heart was left too long in the snow, and no amount of rubbing or friction can warm it again.

Tarts and jellies with mercury sublimate; rofalgar mixed in broth; the gamey flavour of your mouth; the sound of your suspirations are like those of a knife being sharpened.

DISCIPLINE

Discipline is primordially ugly—your disciplines, take them, for they are useless in this place. Did you hear of that old Roman general who would cut off the hands of deserters and cast them about to instill fear into his legionnaires?

And when those veterans returned home, unable to grasp a cup, their wives and children wept with shame and from the Temple of Mars they were forbidden.

CALABAR BEAN

The heat was really quite strong, but he was sweating for other reasons really; witchcraft, yes, he had thrown a few curses here and there.

"Eat another bean."

"Must I?"

"Then you admit to your crimes?"

"No!"

"Then another bean you must eat."

The drool drifted from his mouth as a slave ship did from the harbour. What a strange thing is humanity, the humanity of cheetahs and bats, leopards and jackals, of a black-necked spitting cobra from whom you might get better odds.

SEASONED HIS FOOD

Seasoned his food every day with a little ground silver instead of salt, Guy de Comondo did.

He was wealthy, had been born with a full head of hair, despised trimming his finger-nails.

The flavour of silver he admired. After a year his skin gained a soft, metallic hue; and after three he really did look like one of Damián de Castro's candlesticks; and an argentine mane fell down his back.

"Keep your honey," he said, "your puerile drops of liquid gold, and if you want pleasure allow me to feed you my silver milk. I will replace your ugly eyes with opals before making you my Minerva, a manufactured carnal statue that will mirror my sharp face as it swerves towards the oblectation of your knuckles and I entreat the horns of your womb."

SAN PEDRO

San Pedro, you saint at the portal, divine exemplar, green palm without fear—some mescaline of infatuation, some immeasurable patience, bitter lime and blade of chartreuse, how I vomited you in the night and prayed in a China pink citadel clustered with statues of the deep jungle beneath a French sky that relaxed its weight in suffocating fluorescence.

There is more sadness in the world than most people can tolerate. So they don't tolerate it. Shyly they turn away, move down the street.

Don't despise life, inanimate objects, food.

There is a monkey but it doesn't have a body, only a head that sits on a rock. Black and horrified a comedy placed up there to look at the giant grass and brave marmots come and snicker near it—morning it is wrapped in mist—night, subtly gleaming in the dark.

A MAGICIAN

A magician lived in the high mountains. Every day he would go and collect bird droppings from the high cliffs—the droppings of vultures and hawks, swallows and falcons. When he had collected ten thousand pounds he began to cook it down in a large cauldron until he eventually ended up with about eight gallons of dense tar. This he further refined with pine sap until he had two ounces of liquid, which he put in a small phial.

Magicians like mountains like flowers the sun like flowers the sun some souls without bodies maybe never had bodies and the devil has slaves little ants. Witches like mountains like flowers watch out they fly out the window fly out on pitchforks and go to kiss gnomes. Witches like mountains like roses what bodies of butterflies of gnomes wrapping themselves together with attenuated ropes ride on a reed and stealing the semen from dead bodies ride on reeds and like mountains like roses like mountains and tempests in bottles souls without bodies maybe never had bodies and the devil has slaves and the slaves are little ants which play flutes made from hollowed-out human hairs. Magicians like hills like roses wringing hands out comes hail and whispering phasmata and the devil has slaves trimming three hairs from the udder of a cow.

THE VENOMOUS SALIVA

The venomous saliva of the cuttlefish paralyz-
es crabs like the gaze of a gorgon and aplysi-
omorpha will destroy the lungs of men who
ply them from the deep and beware of the
poison dart frog, better you lick the skin of
that Sonoran Desert toad and lay back as the
sky comes and engulfs you or visit cardinal
hells and spirit worlds, steamed in fear, fire
pit of live coals up to knees; stinking carnal
grounds, maggots' home—yes, we sucked
at each other's saliva, and then lay back,
exhausted.

Hating your neighbour, do you poison
your own flowers so that his bees might die?

Peeping in pouches carrying tongues which
taste of wet shagreen some creatures who live
on juice of lichens muttering effigies the skin
of a bison is called a robe splendid worms in
skeins amber fruits hooking such things.

THE GRAIN

The grain that year bled while still on the sheaf and the wine was sour.

"Never mind," said a young woman. "In the forest good herbs grow that we can eat."

And so they gathered these and ate them. They kissed, they laughed, they kissed.

When word got out of their merriment, soldiers came and put them all to the sword.

AT ONE POINT

At one point, the sun ate its own sperm and multiplied until there were ten, and they all waved their arms and baked the earth and dried the rivers, lakes and oceans. Giant snakes started to eat up the people.

Then rain came and drowned almost everyone who was still alive, but once the floods subsided huge skirret plants grew from the earth, filling the fields and plains.

There is a type of lantern that is able to capture stars. Anyone who has one of these never needs to worry about lighting their house at night.

PAPILIONES IN
SORDIBUS

DR. VERATTI

Dr. Veratti drew on his pipe, let out a little puff of smoke, and continued:

"The truth is that the bulk of what Moses wrote, was written in hieroglyphics, an obvious truth since that man, that prophet, was raised as an Egyptian and learned to read and write in their language at the age of ten, in the foremost school of that epoch, which was called the Garden of Eden. Though he is, sadly, only remembered as having composed five books, using his black tears as ink, the truth of the matter is far different, for in all he wrote fifty-two, the forty-second of which is still stored in the Pope's private library in the Vatican, a fact which I can verify, since I saw it with my own eyes sixteen years ago when I was called there to perform certain repairs. . . . It is my opinion, furthermore, that the common books assigned to Moses, that is to say Genesis, Exodus, Leviticus, Numbers and Deuteronomy, underwent significant editing, many years after his demise, by that dabbler Ezra, and in the process of translating them from Egyptian to Hebrew he undoubtedly took more than a few liberties—and thus, to look at the true unadulterated words of the prophet, we must look to those lost books."

They were seated at a café, beneath the arcs of the Piazza della Cisterna. Cars, driven by mathematicians, geometrists, living philosophers, continuously went by, their tires rumbling along the cobblestones. The blue sky, without a cloud, flashed above them.

"The four Adams . . ." Rodolfo Arcano, the concert musician, began, after taking the final sip of his espresso. "The four Adams——"

But hearing the name "Adam" the eyes of Dr. Veratti suddenly expanded, smoke poured out of his thin nostrils, and his voice gained in both volume and range:

"The four Adams simply refer to the four beards—the four beards of man—the four beards of *the* man! . . . The primitive waters of Genesis, beyond a doubt, were composed by Signor Moses with the aid of previously existent documents, again, PURELY EGYPTIAN, that had been written in the remotest periods of the past and that he was, in the temples he wandered in, privy to—and naturally, of course, he had perused that scroll that Melchizedek had written in his ninetieth year, which is to say in his early youth, and which is called *The Creation of Man*. . . . So we might say that Moses himself was not without the propensity of plagiarism—but that does not mean that his compositions were lacking in profound truth. For example, there is the instance when Elzaphan, asked him about birds."

"Oh?"

"The episode exists in the fifteenth book of Moses, which is now vanished, but which was told about in a certain work by Barebreo, a partial copy of which I had the honor to bind two years ago, on the day of San Sozonte.

"'You have a fear of birds?' Moses asked.

"'Yes,' said Elzaphan, 'their wings appear to me to be made of fire; their beaks are blades which seek to excavate my heart. When they scream, I shiver and wish to hide. They circle about overhead and their shadows are like the trampling of iron heels.'

"'This is called misunderstanding,' the prophet replied. 'Birds, which represent the order of the universe, have hatched from the eggs of chaos. Their two wings are good and evil, night and day, and their beaks are the trumpets which signal sudden change—sometimes ubiquitous, sometimes violent. Birds are the rising sun, for they came from the temple of light. They are made from earth and they are made from water.'"

"The birds of the heavens," Arcano murmured, and just then the bells struck three.

". . . a few hours of work before dinner," Dr. Veratti was saying as he rose to his feet. "Allow me," he added, casting a few euros down on the table; and then he was stepping quickly towards the funicular, which would help him descend even further into extravagance, the incantations of intellectual gluttony, the sifting of thoughts and the accumulation of powders.

Rodolfo Arcano was not without his own mental activity.

"Every day," he said to himself, as he flew away, "I have tried to expose to that man the celestial secrets of rapture, but he has sealed my lips with dated gossip. So many references to birds, without once a mention that we were the ones who ate Jesus when he was on the cross."

EVERYONE SUSPECTED HIM

Everyone suspected him of drunkenness—a suspicion that could have been at least partially verified by the fact that he spent an hour each day at the lone bar in the area—a ristorante-bar-pizzeria that existed three hundred meters from the city walls, and served glasses of Sangiovese of the hills at a correct price, and would fill up your empty bottle with the same if you brought one. His hair and beard, once blond, were white, and his hands were stained with green and blue, and his big British body could be seen rolling through town, post-aperitivo; and his accent was like his body: thick and English.

"He's a painter," some would say.

"I am an artist," he, Halliwell Gordon Wyngarde, would say, as if that forgave everything. "I paint poetry."

The paintings he painted were, indeed, poetry. The most romantic landscapes flowed from his brush—purple mountains and pink forests, with green sunrays and glaring yellow grasses. If one looked closely, one might have discerned strange birds floating about in the air, or odd little animals prancing about in the fields. Yes, he was certainly a man who painted in verse, and not prose—painted canvasses that almost rhymed, paintings that were happy song. Fortunately, however, no one needed to buy them, for the family he came from was far from poor—had, it seemed to many, received the benison of the gods.

The place he stayed at was the top floor of the old Palazzo Ferrante-Gonzaga, where the views were breathtaking. The windows were large and when he left them open on summer nights, bats would come swinging through the place, and they said things to him which he seemed to ignore.

People had been tortured in the dungeons of that palace and in the piazza that stood before it, put to death, as the most fabulous sunsets in the world showed themselves. It might be mentioned, also, that four hundred years earlier Caravaggio, having just thrust his dagger into the breast of a man, had been hosted there and, Halliwell Gordon Wyngarde told himself, though he himself was as good a painter as Caravaggio, he could still use a little of that man's magic, and so that was another reason he had planted in that building of old stone his studio, and his bed.

So, poetry, yes, he painted that—but when summer ended, and the bees quit buzzing about their hives, the zone changed, and so did he. Though most of the living men left that distant outpost, the ancient spirits remained, came, gained force.

The rose petals had withered and died, but goats were rutting with dogs in the field. The oaks, elms and beeches had shed their leaves, and the wind lusted around the cypress and the fir; and, on those short days and throughout those long nights, he set to work, to paint the picture of . . . the Queen.

The throne was there as an old memory and he could feel her soft hair and hear her. She sounded like an old hinge.

He had adorned it with poppies and knelt before it, as fragile as foam. That darling, darling, darling . . .

As playful as a top, eyes of wild curiosity, eyes of the moon, eyes of deepest knowledge. And then he became her son—the son of one so much younger than himself—but as ancient as infinity!

He went into the chiesa and gazed at the Madonna there—the apotropaic Madonna of the Mountain, made of wood, said to be a thousand years old—painted like a doll now, dressed in lace, with blonde hair taken from some child long ago and a crown of sorts. He felt a rush of cold moisture and shivered and then turned on his feet. Outside the wind swept through his hair, penetrated his beard, and intelligence seemed to come to him, slithering like a serpent from its cavern.

He begged her to eat the rats in his head, to drive them away.

His pallet had become a bubbling cauldron into which he dipped deeply his brush, applying that magic potion of paint to a surface that seemed to always be moving, that he seemed to be needing to catch.

Each day brought with it new revelations in color and shade and he looked with strange perception. The walls were mountains, the mountains were walls. And it came to pass that the grand door of the fortification opened and when he went within he saw that it was full of little phantoms groping, teeth chattering, hair of needles bristling.

"If you wish your work to be put on exhibition in the Gallery of Hell, you had better work harder, my lad!"

Mercury and the moon spun about in the sky; fogs filled the valleys below; in the ossuary of the church the bones gave off a succession of short, sharp sounds.

"Your destiny has been divulged and your retinas unlocked. Reversed virgins, flaming rods, dragons and angry boars. Drench your mouth in wine and your organ in sappy fluid. Now, in this ultimate genre, you can free yourself of the orgasms of the ancient Pompeians and impotent Georgian iconography. You are travelling the path of this priesthood and abandoning all optical regulations. Never think that your pubescent slaughter has been forgotten."

"No."

"You burnt your brothers, my hundred thousand sons, and sold them as fertilizer—tarnishing my vulva with manure."

"Should I hang myself?"

"Worms crawl; bugs crawl; painters paint."

Her teeth he made as sharp as he could and her ears were amulets and her aegis was as violent as any war, as any disaster. He studded the picture with slashes of gore and of gold, lustrated her knee with a queer monkey playing a flute—or was it he—was that face his, was it the face of Halliwell Gordon Wyngarde, an intoxicated ape? . . . Did he too have paws?

In any case, the next day dead pigeons appeared on the piazza, their throats and breasts red and torn. Had her fury been poured upon them?

Her portrait! Her portrait!

And he would paint even when his eyes were shut. Is all he saw was her. It was, after all, his ten fingers which had helped her in her divinity, and had helped her board the royal barque. He slurped down wine and spewed rainbows of hawks and wasps; articulated the facial features; squeezed epiphany out of a tube and searched for cosmic order in the raging gyrations of his brush; that ferocious interaction, that hysteria, those night demons that were causing him to spit out bitterness and sourness from that awful wound that was his mouth. . . .

And then the sun's heat . . .

"And who is he?" someone asked when June came.

"A painter—a romantic painter—a painter of poetry and of light."

"He seems a bit . . ."

"Drunk? . . . But of course, these artists, and especially the English, are all eccentrics."

"Yes."

"And . . . *le belle donne* . . ."

THERE WERE WHITE CLOUDS

There were white clouds in the sky, but he, Quilichino, had his own white clouds—on the earth—clouds that grazed on the grass, gave him wool for his clothes, milk for his cheese, meat for his table.

"You have the finest flock," others said when they saw him.

But he dared not even nod, dared not visibly agree, for he felt that he was too fortunate—and, indeed, good fortune is only a mask for another kind of face.

And so it was that when he saw, come from the sky, a hand of strength reach out and take one of his sheep and crush it, he was more sorrowful than astounded. The voices of people, the impure voices of men, had reached the ears of others—a demon, an angel, he could not say what it was. He burnt the bloody animal and prayed to God, and that night it rained, and he felt that perhaps his bad luck had passed.

But what man with lice in his beard is able to keep it?

And so it happened that, before the sun had risen and set many times, that large hand came again, and taking one, two, three members of the flock of Quilichino, destroyed them, and those that remained wailed—wailed so that tears came to the eyes of Quilichino.

"They are as harmless and white as doves," he said in his sorrow, "and yet are being crushed like creeping serpents."

And he was afraid.

"If you wish to resolve your problems," he was told, "you must visit Alcadino the Cricket, for that man understands all things."

Quilichino hesitated one day and then two, three black nights and then four, but then it came that his flock was diminished further and his terror increased, and so he went to Alcadino the Cricket and begged him for his help. That man, who had become drunk on the philosophic sciences, existed in a windowless place made of stone, a place in which there was smoke from fires and wild herbs and garlands of dried frogs hung.

"The hand of destiny is strong, the hand of man is weak," Alcadino said. "Though you are a shepherd, you are not one of the Seven Shepherds. Only you know your true intent, your true desire."

And then Alcadino the Cricket told him what he must do, and it happened that the next day he, Quilichino, took a sharpened ax to one sheep after another until their vital fluid became a brook, but then he had no need to seek revenge on himself.

But it had happened that the Great Lord had put the souls of men into the bodies of the flock.

KARL WAS EXCEEDINGLY TALL

Karl was exceedingly tall. He sometimes had
to duck when entering doorways. His gait was
like that of a stork, a fact made more appar-
ent by him always putting himself in tight
trousers.

Having been lost his whole life, he was
quite pleased when, in his thirty-second year,
at the offices on Wiesenstrasse, he began to
take classes in evolutionary breathing, the
instructor of which was a certain Dr. Sohar, a
being whose face was hidden behind a black
frothy bush, the seeds of which might have
been planted by those kings whose names
were written on bricks.

After the fifth week of group instruction,
the doctor pulled him aside.

"You are a born mystic," he said. "It is
private lessons you will have from this point
forth."

That night Karl dreamed that he was climbing a ladder, the rungs of which were very far apart, so that even with his long legs he was obliged to strain.

"To remedy the evil of your existence," Dr. Sohar said, "you must govern your breathing as if with a whip, ignoring the debased mores of the mortal race. Inhale nine times, exhale once. . . . Exhale twelve times, inhale twice, and enter the zone to which you belong. . . . Inhale through your nose and ears—exhale through your teary eyes! Castigate your lungs, propel oxygen into your spine. The Egyptian posture—that of the universal understanding of Tat. . . . Stick out your rump—push out your chest! Sniff the semen, spit out your voice, transmuting the reproductive energy, and emitting controlling vibrations from the coccyx. Let the motion never cease! . . . And woe to you if you should not practice accordingly!"

Over the next months, the instructions and worthy details he received were profound— bells that rang in his ears and made the worms of his brain jump and crawl. Through new eyes he saw red magma gushing from the pores of the earth; forests burned; the sky was a seeping, glowing vulva. Plates were shifting, and the races of man were chewing on each other's bones—cracking them open and gulping down the marrow. Electrical cannons were booming and the terrible incense of crime wafting through the air!

A tongue was wrapping itself around the globe—and there were so many sounds, so many perceptions, so many reflections.

※

He met a woman. She was ten years older than himself but beautiful, her eyelids caked in powder. They made rapid, tender love and then lay in each other's sweat, their limbs wrapped in gamey aromas.

"I am a widow," she said in her nakedness. "My husband was criminally murdered. His remains rest in the Schosshaldenfriedhof."

"I shall bring him back to you," Karl said nobly, "if that should be your wish."

And, she said, in a voice full of meaning, that it was.

※

What narcotics did he use on her? Impossible to say. The air was full of dark clouds. Things were buzzing and singing and it seemed as if the bars of many cages had been lifted. Did the rungs lead downward now? There was a hole and some venomous fluid seemed to be bubbling within it.

What narcotics did he use on her? It is not easy to say. But he lured a snake from the abyss of that place, and then himself, after being bit on the ankle and raising his hands to heaven, fell down dead.

CURIOUS BIRTHS
TO LIGHT
THE UNIVERSE

THERE WAS A CERTAIN WOMAN

There was a certain woman who, at the age of seventy, began practicing Taoist magic in order to produce a child. After several years, she became pregnant and, after a further eight, gave birth. The baby, however, was made of stone.

A VERY SURPRISING BIRTH

A very surprising birth is that of Mark Adams, who was generated from the refuse of a sewer—from the comingling of fluids flushed by residents of the city. His cries were heard from the street and firemen pulled him from the filth.

Though leading a troubled youth, he later became a prominent businessman, the owner of many exquisite things.

WHEN, IN THE SUMMER

When, in the summer of 1077, Queen Myeongui gave birth to an egg, everyone at the Royal Palace was greatly surprised. The eunuchs were summoned and, one by one, each took their turn sitting on it. When it hatched, however, the child was found to be a female, and therefore not eligible as an heir to the throne. It was said that the Queen had great affection for the girl.

JOCHEN

Jochen was an artist. He had studied at the Kunstakademie Münster and the Kunstakademie Düsseldorf and his work was shown at the Galerie Kleindienst in Leipzig.

He was greatly fond of stones. Every morning he would go for a walk, in the fields and along the wooded pathways near his residence, and it was his habit, during this activity, to pick up a small stone, caress it, and put it in his pocket.

One day he did this, picking up an attractive stone at the beginning of his walk and putting it in his pocket. But, after fifteen minutes, he saw another, equally attractive, and deposited it in the same pocket.

When he got home and emptied the contents of his pocket, however, he found to his surprise that there were not only the two stones but also a shiny little pebble.

IN NIGERIA

In Nigeria, in the General Hospital at Kubwa, Abuja, a girl was born with a long poem written on her body, in the French language. The only one present who could read the poem was a nurse by the name of Helen Kosoko. Upon being questioned, the mother reported that, during her pregnancy, she often dreamed that a thin white man with short hair and a moustache would stand before her and speak of both love and suffering.

IN ITALY

In Italy, in the year 1756, bandits killed a priest by the name of Arlotto Gelmini, while the latter was travelling from Rome to Assisi. As the incident occurred in the lonely hills of Umbria, during the hot month of July, when few venture far from their dwellings without exceptionally good reason, it came that his body was not soon discovered.

In the heat, the body soon began to rot and fester—and from this mound of rotting flesh, a child was born and the child subsisted on the rotting flesh of its host until Autumn came, at which time it was discovered by a hunter.

The child's sex, however, was impossible to determine.

THIS HAPPENED

This happened a long time ago, in Irapuato, Mexico.

Old Man Gonzales was not very large. So, when he climbed into the womb of Ninel Herrera, the owner of a modest pensión on Av. Juan José Torres Landa, it was not terribly difficult. She was asleep, lying in a soccer field near the edge of town when it happened. She was no virgin, but, all the same, was rather surprised when she found herself pregnant. It was almost two years before she gave birth.

SOFIA BJERKEROT

Sofia Bjerkerot, not entirely sure who the father was, gave birth to Aliette. She came out looking like a woman of around forty-five years, with a full head of hair, black and grey. After sixty-three days, the child gave birth to a baby of her own, as large as herself, which the grandmother named Ika.

IT IS SAID

It is said that one who steals cotton clothing is reborn as a crane; one who steals rice is reborn as a cat; one who steals honey is reborn as a gnat; one who steals perfume is reborn as a mole; one who steals fried pies is reborn as an ant.

A man by the name of Bank Roshan did all of the above.

Spontaneously he was born from a hole in the ground—with the wings of a crane, the teeth of a cat, a body like that of a gnat, the eyes of a mole, and the legs of an ant.

IN THE DISTANT PAST

In the distant past a purple vapor lingered about, drifting this way and that, expanding and contracting and expanding—moving and staying still, moving and staying still; and staying still. Eventually it congealed and remained that way for many thousands of years and from it Mu Kung was born.

To gain approval, make an offering.

JUANITA FRANCISCELLA

Juanita Franciscella was born in the city of Castile in the year 1461, to a woman who divided her time between brujería and prostitution, and a barber, Estebanillo by name. Truth be told, they did not at first know if they should not name her Juan, for the child had as much male as female to her person and, when she grew to maturity, there was nothing lacking of either sex about her and from her chin grew a beard no less than six inches in length. Her father was always trying to get her to let him shave it, but she refused and became a street performer of some renown, proficient in the arts of both juggling and playing the citole; both reciting poetry and displaying minor feats of acrobatics.

In 1483, she gave birth to a male child and, when she brought it to her father to see, the latter said, "So, you have turned out just like your mother—having a baby out of wedlock, just as she did with you. And so who, might I ask, is this poor baby's father?"

"This child's father," Juanita replied, "loves it and will care for it as much as its mother. And how could the father and mother be united in matrimony, when they are the same person, as the Lord gave with his creation? For the father is no other than I, who am as well the mother, and I am indeed an honorable virgin, for no other man has had me but me."

JIANG YUAN

Jiang Yuan, the wife of Emperor Ku, was unable to conceive. Her mother-in-law constantly berated her, calling her a useless girl.

Jiang Yuan, feeling extremely embarrassed by the situation, took special herbs from faraway places that were reputed to help, and summoned doctors and magicians, but still, she remained childless. She felt oppressed by the walls of her chamber, the remarks of her mother-in-law, the displeased gazes of her husband, and began, frequently, to wander off into the countryside.

One day she came across a giant footprint, which had been left by Shang Ti. Filled with delight, she jumped into the footprint, walked from one end to the other and then lay down and fell asleep. When she awoke, she felt something stirring inside her and, nine months later, she gave birth to Hou Ji.

MARGARET

Margaret, the daughter of William I, the Count of Holland, at forty-two years of age, on a Good Friday in the year 1276, gave birth to three hundred and sixty-five very small children. One hundred and eighty-two were male, one hundred and eighty-two female, and one of them was a hermaphrodite. They were christened in two basins at the church of Loosduinen, all the males being given the name of Jan, and all the females that of Elizabeth, while the single hermaphrodite received the name of Fran. The mother and all the children, apart from the hermaphrodite, died shortly thereafter. Most of the children were buried inside the church, but the doctor who presided over the strange birth set aside twenty-nine, which he sold to certain wealthy individuals around Europe.

Five were later kept in a glass jar by Emperor Charles V and were, in fact, one of the most prized showpieces of his establishment.

A BRAHMIN WOMAN

A brahmin woman by the name of Anupama was very fond of drinking alcohol. When her guru found out about this habit of hers, he was quite displeased.

"You will have to perform an expiatory rite," he said.

"And what is that?" she asked.

"First you will have to drink semen."

"And then?"

"You will have to eat feces."

"And . . . ?"

"And then you must drink a cup of cow's urine."

Anupama, however, did not heed the guru's words and was, therefore, in due time, reborn as a vulture from the womb of a pig.

AN OLD WOMAN

An old woman was by the river's edge washing clothes when a giant peach came floating along. She retrieved it from the water and brought it home.

"That is the biggest peach I have ever seen!" her husband, who was even older than her, said.

"Shall we?"

"Yes!"

They cut into the peach in order to eat it, but inside found a baby boy. As they had no children of their own, they were quite pleased and raised it, and the boy was named Tarō.

When he grew up, he got married to a very attractive lady by the name of Kiyoko and after that, each year, for seven years, Kiyoko gave birth to a peach, each one more sweet than the last.

OTTO HELM

Otto Helm, acrobat, married his wife Lillian, of the same occupation, on the 14th of August, 1872, in the ring of the Circus Renz, in Berlin.

The two were as in love with each other as they were their art.

Often, when the other performers had retired for the night, the amorous couple would continue practicing their routine—sometimes snatching kisses as they flew past each other on the trapeze—casting lustful glances—inciting desire, one into the next. On a few occasions, they went about their exercises completely unclothed and it was in such a manner that Lillian became pregnant—the child being conceived as the two twisted and coiled from the rigging.

Despite a doctor's warnings and the protestations of the circus manager, Lillian continued to work throughout the period of gestation. And it was, while she was performing her famous aerial hoop act, that she, in fact, gave birth, the child falling onto the safety net below.

ON MAY 12TH, 1974

On May 12th, 1974, in Paradise, California, a woman gave birth to a firefly.

AT THE AGE OF NINETEEN

At the age of nineteen, in the city of Guangzhou, Chen Jin decided that the best way to advance himself in life was to become a eunuch. For, by this method, and a few well-placed bribes, he might enter the royal palace and live a life of ease.

He therefore went to a doctor known for his expertise in such things and was given much strong drink, so that he might be relaxed and to lessen the pain, and the doctor drank much too, and so soon after the task was completed, they were both unconscious. It was at this point that a bitch from the street wandered in, took up the freshly-severed genitals, and made off, believing that it would have itself a savory meal. A passerby, however, saw the dog with something bloody in its mouth and, deciding that it had stolen some meat, hit the beast with a stick, causing it to drop its load, which then fell into the waterway, where it floated along until it was picked up by the occupant of a certain flower boat and used for carnal purposes, the lady in question taking no precautions, her thinking that, as it was disembodied, none were needed.

And it was from this incident that a male child was born, who came to be known as Wins the Magic.

SALKHAJI

Salkhaji was an unsavory character. He regularly criticized good and praised evil; he lied and stole; he was guilty of murder and often engaged in violent activity.

After doing all this, he committed one of the five parallel actions of immediate retribution—that is, he killed an arhat, resulting in him immediately being bound for rebirth in hell as an incandescent being. Through the incomprehensible laws of the working of nature, however, his accumulated karma from some of the previous acts mentioned destined him first to have an intermediate existence as the offspring of a dog. So, through the complications of cause and effect, the incandescent embryo was deposited in the womb of a dog, thus burning its way out of the animal.

IN THE ABBEY

In the Abbey of Santa María la Real de Las Huelgas there lived a nun by the name of María López de Vergós. Devoted especially to Christ, she shut herself in her chamber and engaged herself in prayer both day and night, not admitting anyone and only allowing water and bread to be given to her through a hole in the door. Strangely, after nine years, she gave birth to a child, a boy, who was born with bleeding holes in both his hands and feet. Unfortunately, the child was killed at the age of six by a wild boar.

A PRETTY MAIDEN

A pretty maiden by the name of Erato would nightly visit the precincts around the temple of Hera in Olympia, where statues of the athletes were erected. After about six months of this activity, she was found to be pregnant. Her parents demanded to know who the father was and she declared that it was the statue of Xenarkes, the all-in fighter. And it was true, for the child grew to look exactly like him.

IN ENGLAND

In England a great many years ago there was a highwayman, James Hind, who for a good period had a rather successful career. One morning, as he was riding his horse near the edge of the town of Hatfield, he saw a woman standing begging by the side of the road, holding a baby to her breast. As it was his habit to give money to the poor, just as it was his to take it from the rich, he gave the woman five shillings, upon which she said that she would return the favor by telling him his fate, and so he showed her his hand.

"You are a kind man," said she, "so it grieves me to tell you that many more years you will not live."

"And how shall I die?"

"As a criminal."

"And how might I live?"

"The only way dead men live is through their offspring."

"I have none."

The woman then took her breast, which the baby had been sucking, and squirted milk on Hind, and then she swatted the back of his horse and he rode away.

Some time after this, he was captured and, in the city of Worcester, received his punishment, which is to say that he was hung, drawn and quartered.

His head was put on display at Bridge Gate and his four quarters at four of the other city gates. The next day though, the quarters and head were no longer there and in their place were five male infants, each covered in blood and howling loudly.

IN JAPAN

In Japan, during the time of Emperor Go-Murakami, there was a bamboo cutter, Gorō by name. He was too poor to visit prostitutes and he was so ugly that no woman would have anything to do with him, so he got into the habit of having sex with bamboo after he had cut it. He left the deposits of his lust in a great many bamboo stalks and in one of these a small female child grew. Gorō tried to raise it, but after three years, the little girl ran away.

THE ORACLE AT DELPHI

The oracle at Delphi told the Messenians that they must sacrifice a virgin to the gods, and so it came to pass that Aristodemos offered his own daughter, Asteropeia, for the purpose, but a young man whose name the pens of poets have not recorded came forward and said that the girl and he were engaged to be married, and therefore she should be spared. But when Aristodemos would not hear his plea, this fellow went further, and lied, claiming that Asteropeia was pregnant with his child. At this Aristodemos became greatly angered and slaughtered his daughter and cut open her womb, to prove the young man's lie. Inside, however, there was a baby, though whose it was no one could guess, for the young lady had never been violated, and even the so-called lover admitted his lie amidst his tears.

The child was Aristomenes and he grew up to be a great hero.

SHOUKRY

Shoukry was the most beautiful youth anyone had ever seen. His eyes were wide and
of a delicacy that was only outdone by his
mouth, the lips of which were even more
finely carved than his eyelids, which seemed
as if they were the craftsmanship of djinn or
gods. His hair was black and slightly curly,
and ringlets fell over his shell-like ears, the
lobes of which had pretty earrings installed
upon them. Many young women had lust
for him, but in them he showed no interest.
Compared to himself, they all seemed rough
and ill-formed.

One day, while hunting, he came across a
pool of good water, shaded by date palms and
fringed with sedge. Feeling thirsty, he knelt
near the pool and bent over to drink from its
waters. Seeing his own reflection, however, he

became suddenly filled with erotic desire and soon his semen flowed into the water.

From this a child was born—a girl who came to be known as Umm,—and it was her that Shoukry eventually wed.

NINIEK

Niniek went to bathe in a clear pool not far from her home. After she had done so, she lay down naked on the rocks in the sun. In this position, a bird flew into her womb and, nine months later, she gave birth.

Did the child have feathers?

A PARTIAL LIST OF SNUGGLY BOOKS

G. ALBERT AURIER *Elsewhere and Other Stories*
CHARLES BARBARA *My Lunatic Asylum*
S. HEZOLNRY BERTHOUD *Misanthropic Tales*
LÉON BLOY *The Tarantulas' Parlor and Other Unkind Tales*
ÉLÉMIR BOURGES *The Twilight of the Gods*
CYRIEL BUYSSE *The Aunts*
JAMES CHAMPAGNE *Harlem Smoke*
FÉLICIEN CHAMPSAUR *The Latin Orgy*
BRENDAN CONNELL *Metrophilias*
BRENDAN CONNELL *Unofficial History of Pi Wei*
BRENDAN CONNELL (editor)
   The Zinzolin Book of Occult fiction
RAFAELA CONTRERAS *The Turquoise Ring and Other Stories*
DANIEL CORRICK (editor)
   Ghosts and Robbers: An Anthology of German Gothic Fiction
ADOLFO COUVE *When I Think of My Missing Head*
QUENTIN S. CRISP *Aiaigasa*
LUCIE DELARUE-MARDRUS *The Last Siren and Other Stories*
LADY DILKE *The Outcast Spirit and Other Stories*
CATHERINE DOUSTEYSSIER-KHOZE
   The Beauty of the Death Cap
ÉDOUARD DUJARDIN *Hauntings*
BERIT ELLINGSEN *Now We Can See the Moon*
ERCKMANN-CHATRIAN *A Malediction*
ALPHONSE ESQUIROS *The Enchanted Castle*
ENRIQUE GÓMEZ CARRILLO *Sentimental Stories*
DELPHI FABRICE *Flowers of Ether*
DELPHI FABRICE *The Red Sorcerer*
DELPHI FABRICE *The Red Spider*
BENJAMIN GASTINEAU *The Reign of Satan*
EDMOND AND JULES DE GONCOURT *Manette Salomon*
REMY DE GOURMONT *From a Faraway Land*
REMY DE GOURMONT *Morose Vignettes*
GUIDO GOZZANO *Alcina and Other Stories*
GUSTAVE GUICHES *The Modesty of Sodom*
EDWARD HERON-ALLEN *The Complete Shorter Fiction*
EDWARD HERON-ALLEN *Three Ghost-Written Novels*